It was early in the winter that Whitefoot found a little hole in a corner of Farmer Brown's sugar-house. *See page 2.*

DOVER
☆ CHILDREN'S THRIFT CLASSICS

Whitefoot the Wood Mouse

THORNTON W. BURGESS

Original Illustrations by Harrison Cady

PUBLISHED IN ASSOCIATION WITH THE
THORNTON W. BURGESS MUSEUM AND THE
GREEN BRIAR NATURE CENTER, SANDWICH, MASSACHUSETTS,
BY
DOVER PUBLICATIONS, INC., MINEOLA, NEW YORK

DOVER CHILDREN'S THRIFT CLASSICS
EDITOR OF THIS VOLUME: JANET BAINE KOPITO

Bibliographical Note

This Dover edition, first published in 2006 in association with the Thornton W. Burgess Museum and the Green Briar Nature Center, Sandwich, Massachusetts, who have provided a new introduction, is an unabridged republication of the work first published by Little, Brown, and Company, Boston, in 1922. It contains the original Harrison Cady illustrations.

Library of Congress Cataloging-in-Publication Data

Burgess, Thornton W. (Thornton Waldo), 1874–1965.
  [Whitefoot, the wood mouse]
  The adventures of Whitefoot the woodmouse / Thornton W. Burgess ; original illustrations by Harrison Cody.
    p. cm. — (Dover children's thrift classics)
  "Published in association with the Thornton W. Burgess Museum and the Green Briar Nature Center, Sandwich, Massachusetts."
  Summary: Whitefoot the wood mouse spends a busy year in the Great Forest trying to find a safe home and avoiding his enemies.
  ISBN 0-486-44944-0 (pbk.)
  [1. Mice—Fiction. 2. Forest animals—Fiction. 3. Survival—Fiction. 4. Forests and forestry—Fiction.] I. Cady, Harrison, 1877– ill. II. Title. III. Series.

PZ7.B917Am 2006
[Fic]—dc22

2005056932

Manufactured in the United States of America
Dover Publications, Inc., 31 East 2nd Street, Mineola, N.Y. 11501

Introduction to the Dover Edition

Whitefoot the Wood Mouse has a lot of things to worry about. You see, he has many enemies, and folks like Hooty the Owl, Yowler the Bob Cat, Old Man Coyote, Reddy Fox, Terror the Goshawk, Shadow the Weasel, Billy Mink, Blacky the Crow, Sammy Jay, Buster Bear, and even Jimmy Skunk would like to eat a plump little wood mouse for dinner! This makes Whitefoot very nervous. He is always looking over his shoulder and darting here and there to avoid his enemies. In this charming book, Whitefoot searches for a new home as he tries to keep away from Shadow the Weasel and Hooty the Owl. Along the way, he meets Little Miss Dainty and finds out what the most beautiful thing in the world is. Little Miss Dainty has a very special surprise for Whitefoot—one that makes him very proud.

Whitefoot the Wood Mouse was written back in 1922. It was part of the Green Forest series of books by Thornton W. Burgess. Mr. Burgess wrote more than 170 books for children. These included many series, such as the Adventure series, the Smiling Pool series, the Green Forest series, the Green Meadow series, the Boy Scout books, the

Wishing-Stone series, and the Old Mother West Wind series. Mr. Burgess wrote many books about birds, animals, flowers, and the seashore. He worked with several different artists to illustrate his books. Harrison Cady, who did the illustrations for *Whitefoot the Wood Mouse,* was associated with Mr. Burgess for over fifty years. Mr. Burgess educated generations of children about the natural world through these entertaining books.

Today, the Thornton W. Burgess Society, a nonprofit environmental-education organization, continues to teach children and adults about the wonders of nature. The Society has three locations in Sandwich, Massachusetts, the birthplace of Thornton Burgess. We invite you to visit us. You can learn more about the Society and about Thornton W. Burgess by visiting our web site: **www.thorntonburgess.org**.

Contents

List of Illustrations

Whitefoot
the Wood Mouse

I.
Whitefoot Spends a Happy Winter

IN all his short life Whitefoot the Wood Mouse never had spent such a happy winter. Whitefoot is one of those wise little people who never allow unpleasant things of the past to spoil their present happiness, and who never borrow trouble from the future. Whitefoot believes in getting the most from the present. The things which are past are past, and that is all there is to it. There is no use in thinking about them. As for the things of the future, it will be time enough to think about them when they happen.

If you and I had as many things to worry about as does Whitefoot the Wood Mouse, we probably never would be happy at all. But Whitefoot is happy whenever he has a chance to be, and in this he is wiser than most human beings. You see, there is not one of all the little people in the Green Forest who has so many enemies to watch out for as has Whitefoot. There are ever so many who would like nothing better than to dine on plump little Whitefoot. There are Buster Bear and Billy Mink and Shadow the Weasel and Unc' Billy Possum and Hooty the Owl and all the members of the Hawk family, not to mention Blacky the Crow in times

1

when other food is scarce. Reddy and Granny Fox and Old Man Coyote are always looking for him.

So you see Whitefoot never knows at what instant he may have to run for his life. That is why he is such a timid little fellow and is always running away at the least little unexpected sound. In spite of all this he is a happy little chap.

It was early in the winter that Whitefoot found a little hole in a corner of Farmer Brown's sugar-house and crept inside to see what it was like in there. It didn't take him long to decide that it was the most delightful place he ever had found. He promptly decided to move in and spend the winter. In one end of the sugar-house was a pile of wood. Down under this Whitefoot made himself a warm, comfortable nest. It was a regular castle to Whitefoot. He moved over to it the store of seeds he had laid up for winter use.

Not one of his enemies ever thought of visiting the sugar-house in search of Whitefoot, and they wouldn't have been able to get in if they had. When rough Brother North Wind howled outside, and sleet and snow were making other little people shiver, Whitefoot was warm and comfortable. There was all the room he needed or wanted in which to run about and play. He could go outside when he chose to, but he didn't choose to very often. For days at a time he didn't have a single fright. Yes indeed, Whitefoot spent a happy winter.

II.
Whitefoot Sees Queer Things

WHITEFOOT had spent the winter undisturbed in Farmer Brown's sugar-house. He had almost forgotten the meaning of fear. He had come to look on that sugar-house as belonging to him. It wasn't until Farmer Brown's boy came over to prepare things for sugaring that Whitefoot got a single real fright. The instant Farmer Brown's boy opened the door, Whitefoot scampered down under the pile of wood to his snug little nest, and there he lay, listening to the strange sounds. At last he could stand it no longer and crept to a place where he could peep out and see what was going on. It didn't take him long to discover that this great two-legged creature was not looking for him, and right away he felt better. After a while Farmer Brown's boy went away, and Whitefoot had the little sugar-house to himself again.

But Farmer Brown's boy had carelessly left the door wide open. Whitefoot didn't like that open door. It made him nervous. There was nothing to prevent those who hunt him from walking right in. So the rest of that night Whitefoot felt uncomfortable and anxious.

He felt still more anxious when next day Farmer

Brown's boy returned and became very busy putting things to right. Then Farmer Brown himself came and strange things began to happen. It became as warm as in summer. You see Farmer Brown had built a fire under the evaporator. Whitefoot's curiosity kept him at a place where he could peep out and watch all that was done. He saw Farmer Brown and Farmer Brown's boy pour pails of sap into a great pan. By and by a delicious odor filled the sugar-house. It didn't take him a great while to discover that these two-legged creatures were so busy that he had nothing to fear from them, and so he crept out to watch. He saw them draw the golden syrup from one end of the evaporator and fill shining tin cans with it. Day after day they did the same thing. At night when they had left and all was quiet inside the sugar-house, Whitefoot stole out and found delicious crumbs where they had eaten their lunch. He tasted that thick golden stuff and found it sweet and good. Later he watched them make sugar and nearly made himself sick that night when they had gone home, for they had left some of that sugar where he could get at it. He didn't understand these queer doings at all. But he was no longer afraid.

III.
Farmer Brown's Boy Becomes Acquainted

IT didn't take Farmer Brown's boy long to discover that Whitefoot the Wood Mouse was living in the little sugar-house. He caught glimpses of Whitefoot peeping out at him. Now Farmer Brown's boy is wise in the ways of the little people of the Green Forest. Right away he made up his mind to get acquainted with Whitefoot. He knew that not in all the Green Forest is there a more timid little fellow than Whitefoot, and he thought it would be a fine thing to be able to win the confidence of such a shy little chap.

So at first Farmer Brown's boy paid no attention whatever to Whitefoot. He took care that Whitefoot shouldn't even know that he had been seen. Every day when he ate his lunch, Farmer Brown's boy scattered a lot of crumbs close to the pile of wood under which Whitefoot had made his home. Then he and Farmer Brown would go out to collect sap. When they returned not a crumb would be left.

One day Farmer Brown's boy scattered some particularly delicious crumbs. Then, instead of going out, he sat down on a bench and kept perfectly still. Farmer Brown and Bowser the Hound went out. Of course Whitefoot heard them go out, and right away he poked his little head out from under the pile of wood to see if the way was clear. Farmer Brown's boy sat there right in plain sight, but Whitefoot didn't see him. That was because Farmer Brown's boy didn't move the least bit. Whitefoot ran out and at once began to eat those delicious crumbs. When he had filled his little stomach, he began to carry the remainder back to his storehouse underneath the woodpile. While he was gone on one of these trips, Farmer Brown's boy scattered more crumbs in a line that led right up to his foot. Right there he placed a big piece of bread crust.

Whitefoot was working so hard and so fast to get all those delicious bits of food that he took no notice of anything else until he reached that piece of crust. Then he happened to look up right into the eyes of Farmer Brown's boy. With a frightened little squeak Whitefoot darted back, and for a long time he was afraid to come out again.

But Farmer Brown's boy didn't move, and at last Whitefoot could stand the temptation no longer. He darted out halfway, scurried back, came out again, and at last ventured right up to the crust. Then he began to drag it back to the woodpile. Still Farmer Brown's boy did not move.

For two or three days the same thing happened. By this time, Whitefoot had lost all fear. He knew that Farmer Brown's boy would not harm him, and it was not long before he ventured to take a bit of food from Farmer Brown's boy's hand. After that Farmer Brown's boy took care that no crumbs should be scattered on the ground. Whitefoot had to come to him for his food, and always Farmer Brown's boy had something delicious for him.

IV.
Whitefoot Grows Anxious

'Tis sad indeed to trust a friend
Then have that trust abruptly end.
Whitefoot.

I know of nothing that is more sad than to feel that a friend is no longer to be trusted. There came a time when Whitefoot the Wood Mouse almost had this feeling. It was a very, very anxious time for Whitefoot.

You see, Whitefoot and Farmer Brown's boy had become the very best of friends there in the little sugar-house. They had become such good friends that Whitefoot did not hesitate to take food from the hands of Farmer Brown's boy. Never in all his life had he had so much to eat or such good things to eat. He was getting so fat that his handsome little coat was uncomfortably tight. He ran about fearlessly while Farmer Brown and Farmer Brown's boy were making maple syrup and maple sugar. He had even lost his fear of Bowser the Hound, for Bowser had paid no attention to him whatever.

Now you remember that Whitefoot had made his home way down beneath the great pile of wood in the sugar-house. Of course Farmer Brown and

8

Farmer Brown's boy used that wood for the fire to boil the sap to make the syrup and sugar. White-foot thought nothing of this until one day he discovered that his little home was no longer as dark as it had been. A little ray of light crept down between the sticks. Presently another little ray of light crept down between the sticks.

It was then that Whitefoot began to grow anxious. It was then he realized that that pile of wood was growing smaller and smaller, and if it kept on growing smaller, by and by there wouldn't be any pile of wood and his little home wouldn't be hidden at all. Of course Whitefoot didn't understand why that wood was slipping away. In spite of himself he began to grow suspicious. He couldn't think of any reason why that wood should be taken away, unless it was to look for his little home. Farmer Brown's boy was just as kind and friendly as ever, but all the time more and more light crept in, as the wood vanished.

"Oh dear, what does it mean?" cried Whitefoot to himself. "They must be looking for my home, yet they have been so good to me that it is hard to believe they mean any harm. I do hope they will stop taking this wood away. I won't have any hiding-place at all, and then I will have to go outside back to my old home in the hollow stump. I don't want to do that. Oh, dear! Oh, dear! I was so happy and now I am so worried! Why can't happy times last always?"

V.
The End of Whitefoot's Worries

You never can tell! You never can tell!
Things going wrong will often end well.
                                    Whitefoot.

THE next time you meet him just ask Whitefoot
if this isn't so. Things had been going very
wrong for Whitefoot. It had begun to look to Whitefoot as if he would no longer have a snug, hidden
little home in Farmer Brown's sugar-house. The
pile of wood under which he had made that snug
little home was disappearing so fast that it began
to look as if in a little while there would be no
wood at all.

Whitefoot quite lost his appetite. He no longer
came out to take food from Farmer Brown's boy's
hand. He stayed right in his snug little home and
worried.

Now Farmer Brown's boy had not once thought
of the trouble he was making. He wondered what
had become of Whitefoot, and in his turn he began
to worry. He was afraid that something had happened to his little friend. He was thinking of this as
he fed the sticks of wood to the fire for boiling the
sap to make syrup and sugar. Finally, as he pulled

10

away two big sticks, he saw something that made him whistle with surprise. It was Whitefoot's nest which he had so cleverly hidden way down underneath that pile of wood when he had first moved into the sugar-house. With a frightened little squeak, Whitefoot ran out, scurried across the little sugar-house and out through the open door.

Farmer Brown's boy understood. He understood perfectly that little people like Whitefoot want their homes hidden away in the dark. "Poor little chap," said Farmer Brown's boy. "He had a regular castle here and we have destroyed it. He's got the snuggest kind of a little nest here, but he won't come back to it so long as it is right out in plain sight. He probably thinks we have been hunting for this little home of his. Hello! Here's his storehouse! I've often wondered how the little rascal could eat so much, but now I understand. He stored away here more than half of the good things I have given him. I am glad he did. If he hadn't, he might not come back, but I feel sure that to-night, when all is quiet, he will come back to take away all his food. I must do something to keep him here."

Farmer Brown's boy sat down to think things over. Then he got an old box and made a little round hole in one end of it. Very carefully he took up Whitefoot's nest and placed it under the old box in the darkest corner of the sugar-house. Then he carried all Whitefoot's supplies over there and put them under the box. He went outside, and got some branches of hemlock and threw these in a little pile over the box. After this he scattered some crumbs just outside.

Late that night Whitefoot did come back. The crumbs led him to the old box. He crept inside. There was his snug little home! All in a second Whitefoot understood, and trust and happiness returned.

VI.
A Very Careless Jump

WHITEFOOT once more was happy. When he found his snug little nest and his store of food under that old box in the darkest corner of Farmer Brown's sugar-house, he knew that Farmer Brown's boy must have placed them there. It was better than the old place under the woodpile. It was the best place for a home Whitefoot ever had had. It didn't take him long to change his mind about leaving the little sugar-house. Somehow he seemed to know right down inside that his home would not again be disturbed.

So he proceeded to rearrange his nest and to put all his supplies of food in one corner of the old box. When everything was placed to suit him he ventured out, for now that he no longer feared Farmer Brown's boy he wanted to see all that was going on. He liked to jump up on the bench where Farmer Brown's boy sometimes sat. He would climb up to where Farmer Brown's boy's coat hung and explore the pockets of it. Once he stole Farmer Brown's boy's handkerchief. He wanted it to add to the material his nest was made of. Farmer Brown's boy discovered it just as it was disappearing, and how he laughed as he pulled it away.

13

So, what with eating and sleeping and playing about, secure in the feeling that no harm could come to him, Whitefoot was happier than ever before in his little life. He knew that Farmer Brown's boy and Farmer Brown and Bowser the Hound were his friends. He knew, too, that so long as they were about, none of his enemies would dare come near. This being so, of course there was nothing to be afraid of. No harm could possibly come to him. At least, that is what Whitefoot thought.

But you know, enemies are not the only dangers to watch out for. Accidents will happen. When they do happen, it is very likely to be when the possibility of them is farthest from your thoughts. Almost always they are due to heedlessness or carelessness. It was heedlessness that got Whitefoot into one of the worst mishaps of his whole life.

He had been running and jumping all around the inside of the little sugar-house. He loves to run and jump, and he had been having just the best time ever. Finally Whitefoot ran along the old bench and jumped from the end of it for a box standing on end, which Farmer Brown's boy sometimes used to sit on. It wasn't a very long jump, but somehow Whitefoot misjudged it. He was heedless, and he didn't jump quite far enough. Right beside that box was a tin pail half filled with sap. Instead of landing on the box, Whitefoot landed with a splash in that pail of sap.

VII.
Whitefoot Gives Up Hope

Whitefoot had been in many tight places. Yes, indeed, Whitefoot had been in many tight places. He had had narrow escapes of all kinds. But never had he felt so utterly hopeless as now.

The moment he landed in that sap, Whitefoot began to swim frantically. He isn't a particularly good swimmer, but he could swim well enough to keep afloat for a while. His first thought was to scramble up the side of the tin pail, but when he reached it and tried to fasten his sharp little claws into it in order to climb, he discovered that he couldn't. Sharp as they were, his little claws just slipped, and his struggles to get up only resulted in tiring him out and in plunging him wholly beneath the sap. He came up choking and gasping. Then round and round inside that pail he paddled, stopping every two or three seconds to try to climb up that hateful, smooth, shiny wall.

The more he tried to climb out, the more frightened he became.

He was in a perfect panic of fear. He quite lost his head, did Whitefoot. The harder he struggled, the more tired he became, and the greater was his danger of drowning.

Whitefoot squeaked pitifully. He didn't want to drown. Of course not. He wanted to live. But unless he could get out of that pail very soon, he would drown. He knew it. He knew that he couldn't hold on much longer. He knew that just as soon as he stopped paddling, he would sink. Already he was so tired from his frantic efforts to escape that it seemed to him that he couldn't hold out any longer. But somehow he kept his legs moving, and so kept afloat.

Just why he kept struggling, Whitefoot couldn't have told. It wasn't because he had any hope. He didn't have the least bit of hope. He knew now that he couldn't climb the sides of that pail, and there was no other way of getting out. Still he kept on paddling. It was the only way to keep from drowning, and though he felt sure that he had got to drown at last, he just wouldn't until he actually had to. And all the time Whitefoot squeaked hopelessly, despairingly, pitifully. He did it without knowing that he did it, just as he kept paddling round and round.

VIII.
The Rescue

WHEN Whitefoot made the heedless jump that landed him in a pail half filled with sap, no one else was in the little sugar-house. Whitefoot was quite alone. You see, Farmer Brown and Farmer Brown's boy were out collecting sap from the trees, and Bowser the Hound was with them.

Farmer Brown's boy was the first to return. He came in just after Whitefoot had given up all hope. He went at once to the fire to put more wood on. As he finished this job he heard the faintest of little squeaks. It was a very pitiful little squeak. Farmer Brown's boy stood perfectly still and listened. He heard it again. He knew right away that it was the voice of Whitefoot.

"Hello!" exclaimed Farmer Brown's boy. "That sounds as if Whitefoot is in trouble of some kind. I wonder where the little rascal is. I wonder what can have happened to him. I must look into this." Again Farmer Brown's boy heard that faint little squeak. It was so faint that he couldn't tell where it came from. Hurriedly and anxiously he looked all over the little sugar-house, stopping every few seconds to listen for that pitiful little squeak. It seemed to come from nowhere in particular. Also it was growing fainter.

At last Farmer Brown's boy happened to stand still close to that tin pail half filled with sap. He heard the faint little squeak again and with it a little splash. It was the sound of the little splash that led him to look down. In a flash he understood what had happened. He saw poor little Whitefoot struggling feebly, and even as he looked Whitefoot's head went under. He was very nearly drowned.

Stooping quickly, Farmer Brown's boy grabbed Whitefoot's long tail and pulled him out. Whitefoot was so nearly drowned that he didn't have strength enough to even kick. A great pity filled the eyes of Farmer Brown's boy as he held Whitefoot's head down and gently shook him. He was trying to shake some of the sap out of Whitefoot. It ran out of Whitefoot's nose and out of his mouth. Whitefoot began to gasp. Then Farmer Brown's boy spread his coat close by the fire, rolled Whitefoot up in his handkerchief and gently placed him on the coat. For some time Whitefoot lay just gasping. But presently his breath came easier, and after a while he was breathing naturally. But he was too weak and tired to move, so he just lay there while Farmer Brown's boy gently stroked his head and told him how sorry he was.

Little by little Whitefoot recovered his strength. At last he could sit up, and finally he began to move about a little, although he was still wobbly on his legs. Farmer Brown's boy put some bits of food where Whitefoot could get them, and as he ate, Whitefoot's beautiful soft eyes were filled with gratitude.

IX.
Two Timid Persons Meet

Thus always you will meet life's test—
To do the thing you can do best.
                              Whitefoot.

JUMPER THE HARE sat crouched at the foot of a
tree in the Green Forest. Had you happened
along there, you would not have seen him. At least,
I doubt if you would. If you had seen him, you probably wouldn't have known it. You see, in his white
coat Jumper was so exactly the color of the snow
that he looked like nothing more than a little heap
of snow.

Just in front of Juniper was a little round hole. He
gave it no attention. It didn't interest him in the
least. All through the Green Forest were little holes
in the snow. Jumper was so used to them that he
seldom noticed them. So he took no notice of this
one until something moved down in that hole.
Jumper's eyes opened a little wider and he
watched. A sharp little face with very bright eyes
filled that little round hole. Jumper moved just the
tiniest bit, and in a flash that sharp little face with
the bright eyes disappeared.

Jumper sat still and waited. After a long wait

the sharp little face with bright eyes appeared again. "Don't be frightened, Whitefoot," said Jumper softly.

At the first word the sharp little face disappeared, but in a moment it was back, and the sharp little eyes were fixed on Jumper suspiciously. After a long stare the suspicion left them, and out of the little round hole came trim little Whitefoot in a soft brown coat with white waistcoat and with white feet and a long, slim tail. This winter he was not living in Farmer Brown's sugar-house.

"Gracious, Jumper, how you did scare me!" said he.

Jumper chuckled. "Whitefoot, I believe you are more timid than I am," he replied.

"Why shouldn't I be? I'm ever so much smaller, and I have more enemies," retorted Whitefoot.

"It is true you are smaller, but I am not so sure that you have more enemies," replied Jumper thoughtfully. "It sometimes seems to me that I couldn't have more, especially in winter."

"Name them," commanded Whitefoot.

"Hooty the Great Horned Owl, Yowler the Bob Cat, Old Man Coyote, Reddy Fox, Terror the Goshawk, Shadow the Weasel, Billy Mink." Jumper paused.

"Is that all?" demanded Whitefoot.

"Isn't that enough?" retorted Jumper rather sharply.

"I have all of those and Blacky the Crow and

Butcher the Shrike and Sammy Jay in winter, and
Buster Bear and Jimmy Skunk and several of the
Snake family in summer," replied Whitefoot. "It
seems to me sometimes as if I need eyes and ears
all over me. Night and day there is always someone
hunting for poor little me. And then some folks
wonder why I am so timid. If I were not as timid as
I am, I wouldn't be alive now; I would have been
caught long ago. Folks may laugh at me for being
so easily frightened, but I don't care. That is what
saves my life a dozen times a day."

Jumper looked interested. "I hadn't thought of
that," said he. "I'm a very timid person myself, and
sometimes I have been ashamed of being so easily
frightened. But come to think of it, I guess you are
right; the more timid I am, the longer I am likely to
live."

Whitefoot suddenly darted into his hole. Jumper
didn't move, but his eyes widened with fear. A
great white bird had just alighted on a stump a
short distance away. It was Whitey the Snowy Owl,
down from the Far North.

"There is another enemy we both forgot,"
thought Jumper, and tried not to shiver.

X.
The White Watchers

Much may be gained by sitting still
If you but have the strength of will.
Whitefoot.

JUMPER THE HARE crouched at the foot of a tree
in the Green Forest, and a little way from him on
a stump sat Whitey the Snowy Owl. Had you been
there to see them, both would have appeared as
white as the snow around them unless you had
looked very closely. Then you might have seen two
narrow black lines back of Jumper's head. They
were the tips of his ears, for these remain black.
And near the upper part of the white mound which
was Whitey you might have seen two round yellow
spots, his eyes.

There they were for all the world like two little
heaps of snow. Jumper didn't move so much as a
hair. Whitey didn't move so much as a feather.
Both were waiting and watching. Jumper didn't
move because he knew that Whitey was there.
Whitey didn't move because he didn't want anyone to know he was there, and didn't know that
Jumper was there. Jumper was sitting still because

he was afraid. Whitey was sitting still because he was hungry.

So there they sat, each in plain sight of the other but only one seeing the other. This was because Jumper had been fortunate enough to see Whitey alight on that stump. Jumper had been sitting still when Whitey arrived, and so those fierce yellow eyes had not yet seen him. But had Jumper so much as lifted one of those long ears, Whitey would have seen, and his great claws would have been reaching for Jumper.

Jumper didn't want to sit still. No, indeed! He wanted to run. You know it is on those long legs of his that Jumper depends almost wholly for safety. But there are times for running and times for sitting still, and this was a time for sitting still. He knew that Whitey didn't know that he was anywhere near. But just the same it was hard, very hard to sit there with one he so greatly feared watching so near. It seemed as if those fierce yellow eyes of Whitey must see him. They seemed to look right through him. They made him shake inside.

"I want to run. I want to run. I want to run," Jumper kept saying to himself. Then he would say, "But I mustn't. I mustn't. I mustn't."

And so Jumper did the hardest thing in the world,—sat still and stared danger in the face. He was sitting still to save his life.

Whitey the Snowy Owl was sitting still to catch a

dinner. I know that sounds queer, but it was so. He knew that so long as he sat still, he was not likely to be seen. It was for this purpose that Old Mother Nature had given him that coat of white. In the Far North, which was his real home, everything is white for months and months, and anyone dressed in a dark suit can be seen a long distance. So Whitey had been given that white coat that he might have a better chance to catch food enough to keep him alive.

And he had learned how to make the best use of it. Yes, indeed, he knew how to make the best use of it. It was by doing just what he was doing now,— sitting perfectly still. Just before he had alighted on that stump he had seen something move at the entrance to a little round hole in the snow. He was sure of it.

"A Mouse," thought Whitey, and alighted on that stump. "He saw me flying, but he'll forget about it after a while and will come out again. He won't see me then if I don't move. And I won't move until he is far enough from that hole for me to catch him before he can get back to it."

So the two watchers in white sat without moving for the longest time, one watching for a dinner and the other watching the other watcher.

XI.
Jumper Is in Doubt

> When doubtful what course to pursue
> 'Tis sometimes best to nothing do.
> *Whitefoot.*

JUMPER THE HARE was beginning to feel easier in his mind. He was no longer shaking inside. In fact, he was beginning to feel quite safe. There he was in plain sight of Whitey the Snowy Owl, sitting motionless on a stump only a short distance away, yet Whitey hadn't seen him. Whitey had looked straight at him many times, but because Jumper had not moved so much as a hair Whitey had mistaken him for a little heap of snow.

"All I have to do is to keep right on sitting perfectly still, and I'll be as safe as if Whitey were nowhere about. Yes, sir, I will," thought Jumper. "By and by he will become tired and fly away. I do hope he'll do that before Whitefoot comes out again. If Whitefoot should come out, I couldn't warn him because that would draw Whitey's attention to me, and he wouldn't look twice at a Wood Mouse when there was a chance to get a Hare for his dinner.

"This is a queer world. It is so. Old Mother

26

Nature does queer things. Here she has given me a white coat in winter so that I may not be easily seen when there is snow on the ground, and at the same time she has given one of those I fear most a white coat so that he may not be easily seen, either. It certainly is a queer world."

Jumper forgot that Whitey was only a chance visitor from the Far North and that it was only once in a great while that he came down there, while up in the Far North where he belonged nearly everybody was dressed in white.

Jumper hadn't moved once, but once in a while Whitey turned his great round head for a look all about in every direction. But it was done in such a way that only eyes watching him sharply would have noticed it. Most of the time he kept his fierce yellow eyes fixed on the little hole in the snow in which Whitefoot had disappeared. You know Whitey can see by day quite as well as any other bird.

Jumper, having stopped worrying about himself, began to worry about Whitefoot. He knew that Whitefoot had seen Whitey arrive on that stump and that was why he had dodged back into his hole and since then had not even poked his nose out. But that had been so long ago that by this time Whitefoot must think that Whitey had gone on about his business, and Jumper expected to see Whitefoot appear any moment. What Jumper didn't know was that Whitefoot's bright little eyes had all the time been watching Whitey from another little hole in the snow some distance away. A tunnel led from this little hole to the first little hole.

Suddenly off among the trees something moved. At least, Jumper thought he saw something move. Yes, there it was, a little black spot moving swiftly this way and that way over the snow. Jumper stared very hard. And then his heart seemed to jump right up in his throat. It did so. He felt as if he would choke. That black spot was the tip end of a tail, the tail of a small, very slim fellow dressed all in white, the only other one in all the Green Forest who dresses all in white. It was Shadow the Weasel! In his white winter coat he is called Ermine.

He was running this way and that way, back and forth, with his nose to the snow. He was hunting, and Jumper knew that sooner or later Shadow would find him. Safety from Shadow lay in making the best possible use of those long legs of his, but to do that would bring Whitey the Owl swooping after him. What to do Jumper didn't know. And so he did nothing. It happened to be the wisest thing he could do.

XII.
Whitey the Owl Saves Jumper

It often happens in the end
An enemy may prove a friend.
Whitefoot.

WAS ever anyone in a worse position than Jumper the Hare? To move would be to give himself away to Whitey the Snowy Owl. If he remained where he was very likely Shadow the Weasel would find him, and the result would be the same as if he were caught by Whitey the Owl. Neither Whitey nor Shadow knew he was there, but it would be only a few minutes before one of them knew it. At least, that is the way it looked to Jumper.

Whitey wouldn't know it unless he moved, but Shadow the Weasel would find his tracks, and his nose would lead him straight there. Back and forth, back and forth, this way, that way and the other way, just a little distance off, Shadow was running with his nose to the snow. He was hunting—hunting for the scent of someone whom he could kill. In a few minutes he would be sure to find where Jumper had been, and then his nose would

29

lead him straight to that tree at the foot of which Jumper was crouching.

Nearer and nearer came Shadow. He was slim and trim and didn't look at all terrible. Yet there was no one in all the Green Forest more feared by the little people in fur, by Jumper, by Peter Rabbit, by Whitefoot, even by Chatterer the Red Squirrel.

"Perhaps," thought Jumper, "he won't find my scent after all. Perhaps he'll go in another direction." But all the time Jumper felt in his bones that Shadow would find that scent. "When he does, I'll run," said Jumper to himself. "I'll have at least a chance to dodge Whitey. I am afraid he will catch me, but I'll have a chance. I won't have any chance at all if Shadow finds me."

Suddenly Shadow stopped running and sat up to look about with fierce little eyes, all the time testing the air with his nose. Jumper's heart sank. He knew that Shadow had caught a faint scent of someone. Then Shadow began to run back and forth once more, but more carefully than before. And then he started straight for where Jumper was crouching! Jumper knew then that Shadow had found his trail.

Jumper drew a long breath and settled his long hind feet for a great jump, hoping to so take Whitey the Owl by surprise that he might be able to get away. And as Jumper did this, he looked over to that stump where Whitey had been sitting so long. Whitey was just leaving it on his great silent wings, and his fierce yellow eyes were fixed in the direction of Shadow the Weasel. He had seen that moving black spot which was the tip of Shadow's tail.

Jumper didn't have time to jump before Whitey was swooping down at Shadow. So Jumper just kept still and watched with eyes almost popping from his head with fear and excitement.

Shadow hadn't seen Whitey until just as Whitey was reaching for him with his great cruel claws. Now if there is anyone who can move more quickly than Shadow the Weasel I don't know who it is. Whitey's claws closed on nothing but snow; Shadow had dodged. Then began a game, Whitey swooping and Shadow dodging, and all the time they were getting farther and farther from where Jumper was.

The instant it was safe to do so, Jumper took to his long heels and the way he disappeared, lipperty-lipperty-lip, was worth seeing. Whitey the Snowy Owl had saved him from Shadow the Weasel and didn't know it. An enemy had proved to be a friend.

XIII.
Whitefoot Decides Quickly

Your mind made up a certain way
Be swift to act; do not delay.
Whitefoot.

WHEN Whitefoot had discovered Whitey the Snowy Owl, he had dodged down in the little hole in the snow beside which he had been sitting. He had not been badly frightened. But he was somewhat upset. Yes, sir, he was somewhat upset. You see, he had so many enemies to watch out for, and here was another.

"Just as if I didn't have troubles enough without having this white robber to add to them," grumbled Whitefoot. "Why doesn't he stay where he belongs, way up in the Far North? It must be that food is scarce up there. Well, now that I know he is here, he will have to be smarter than I think he is to catch me. I hope Jumper the Hare will have sense enough to keep perfectly still. I've sometimes envied him his long legs, but I guess I am better off than he is, at that. Once he has been seen by an enemy, only those long legs of his can save him, but I have a hundred hiding-places down under the snow. Whitey is watching the hole where I disappeared; he thinks I'll come out there again after a while. I'll fool him."

Whitefoot scampered along through a little tunnel and presently very cautiously peeped out of another little round hole in the snow. Sure enough, there was Whitey the Snowy Owl back to him on a stump, watching the hole down which he had disappeared a few minutes before. Whitefoot grinned. Then he looked over to where he had last seen Jumper. Jumper was still there; it was clear that he hadn't moved, and so Whitey hadn't seen him. Again Whitefoot grinned. Then he settled himself to watch patiently for Whitey to become tired of watching that hole and fly away.

So it was that Whitefoot saw all that happened. He saw Whitey suddenly sail out on silent wings from that stump and swoop with great claws reaching for someone. And then he saw who that someone was,—Shadow the Weasel! He saw Shadow dodge in the very nick of time. Then he watched Whitey swoop again and again as Shadow dodged this way and that way. Finally both disappeared amongst the trees. Then he turned just in time to see Jumper the Hare bounding away with all the speed of his wonderful, long legs.

Fear, the greatest fear he had known for a long time, took possession of Whitefoot. "Shadow the Weasel!" he gasped and had such a thing been possible he certainly would have turned pale. "Whitey won't catch him; Shadow is too quick for him. And

He watched Whitey swoop again and again
as Shadow dodged this way and that way. *See page 33*.

when Whitey has given up and flown away, Shadow will come back. He probably had found the tracks of Jumper the Hare and he will come back. I know him; he'll come back. Jumper is safe enough from him now, because he has such a long start, but Shadow will be sure to find one of my holes in the snow. Oh, dear! Oh, dear! What shall I do?"

You see Shadow the Weasel is the one enemy that can follow Whitefoot into most of his hiding-places.

For a minute or two Whitefoot sat there, shaking with fright. Then he made up his mind. "I'll get away from here before he returns," thought Whitefoot. "I've got to. I've spent a comfortable winter here so far, but there will be no safety for me here any longer. I don't know where to go, but anywhere will be better than here now."

Without waiting another second, Whitefoot scampered away. And how he did hope that his scent would have disappeared by the time Shadow returned. If it hadn't, there would be little hope for him and he knew it.

XIV.
Shadow's Return

He little gains and has no pride
Who from his purpose turns aside.
Whitefoot.

SHADOW THE WEASEL believes in persistence. When he sets out to do a thing, he keeps at it until it is done or he knows for a certainty it cannot be done. He is not easily discouraged. This is one reason he is so feared by the little people he delights to hunt. They know that once he gets on their trail, they will be fortunate indeed if they escape him.

When Whitey the Snowy Owl swooped at him and so nearly caught him, he was not afraid as he dodged this way and that way. Any other of the little people with the exception of his cousin, Billy Mink, would have been frightened half to death. But Shadow was simply angry. He was angry that anyone should try to catch him. He was still more angry because his hunt for Jumper the Hare was interfered with. You see, he had just found Jumper's trail when Whitey swooped at him.

So Shadow's little eyes grew red with rage as he dodged this way and that and was gradually driven

36

away from the place where he had found the trail
of Jumper the Hare. At last he saw a hole in an old
log and into this he darted. Whitey couldn't get
him there. Whitey knew this and he knew, too, that
waiting for Shadow to come out again would be a
waste of time. So Whitey promptly flew away.

Hardly had he disappeared when Shadow
popped out of that hole, for he had been peeping
out and watching Whitey. Without a moment's
pause he turned straight back for the place where
he had found the trail of Jumper the Hare. He had
no intention of giving up that hunt just because he
had been driven away. Straight to the very spot
where Whitey had first swooped at him he ran, and
there once more his keen little nose took up the
trail of Jumper. It led him straight to the foot of the
tree where Jumper had crouched so long.

But, as you know, Jumper wasn't there then.
Shadow ran in a circle and presently he found
where Jumper had landed on the snow at the end
of that first bound. Shadow snarled. He understood exactly what had happened.

"Jumper was under that tree when that white
robber from the Far North tried to catch me, and
he took that chance to leave in a hurry. I can tell
that by the length of this jump. Probably he is still
going. It is useless to follow him because he has
too long a start," said Shadow, and he snarled
again in rage and disappointment.

Then, for such is his way, he wasted no more

time or thought on Jumper the Hare. Instead he began to look for other trails. So it was that he found one of the little holes of Whitefoot the Wood Mouse.

"Ha! So this is where Whitefoot has been living this winter!" he exclaimed. Once more his eyes glowed red, but this time with eagerness and the joy of the hunt. He plunged down into that little hole in the snow. Down there the scent of Whitefoot was strong. Shadow followed it until it led out of another little hole in the snow. But there he lost it. You see, it was so long since Whitefoot had hurriedly left that the scent on the surface had disappeared.

Shadow ran swiftly this way and that way in a big circle, but he couldn't find Whitefoot's trail again. Snarling with anger and disappointment, he returned to the little hole in the snow and vanished. Then he followed all Whitefoot's little tunnels. He found Whitefoot's nest. He found his store of seeds. But he didn't find Whitefoot.

"He'll come back," muttered Shadow, and curled up in Whitefoot's nest to wait.

XV.
Whitefoot's Dreadful Journey

Danger may be anywhere,
So I expect it everywhere.
Whitefoot.

WHITEFOOT THE WOOD MOUSE was terribly frightened. Yes, sir, he was terribly frightened. It was a long, long time since he had been as frightened as he now was. He is used to frights, is Whitefoot. He has them every day and every night, but usually they are sudden frights, quickly over and as quickly forgotten.

This fright was different. You see Whitefoot had caught a glimpse of Shadow the Weasel. And he knew that if Shadow returned he would be sure to find the little round holes in the snow that led down to Whitefoot's private little tunnels underneath.

The only thing for Whitefoot to do was to get just as far from that place as he could before Shadow should return. And so poor little Whitefoot started out on a journey that was to take him he knew not where. All he could do was to go and go and go until he could find a safe hiding-place.

My, my, but that was a dreadful journey! Every

time a twig snapped, Whitefoot's heart seemed to jump right up in his throat. Every time he saw a moving shadow, and the branches of the trees moving in the wind were constantly making moving shadows on the snow, he dodged behind a tree trunk or under a piece of bark or wherever he could find a hiding-place.

You see, Whitefoot has so many enemies always looking for him that he hides whenever he sees anything moving. When at home, he is forever dodging in and out of his hiding-places. So, because everything was strange to him, and because of the great fear of Shadow the Weasel, he suspected everything that moved and every sound he heard. For a long way no one saw him, for no one was about. Yet all that way Whitefoot twisted and dodged and darted from place to place and was just as badly frightened as if there had been enemies all about.

"Oh, dear! Oh, dear me!" he kept saying over and over to himself. "Wherever shall I go? Whatever shall I do? However shall I get enough to eat? I won't dare go back to get food from my little store-houses, and I shall have to live in a strange place where I won't know where to look for food. I am getting tired. My legs ache. I'm getting hungry. I want my nice, warm, soft bed. Oh, dear! Oh, dear! Oh, dear me!"

But in spite of his frights, Whitefoot kept on. You see, he was more afraid to stop than he was to go on. He just had to get as far from Shadow the Weasel as he could. Being such a little fellow, what would be a short distance for you or me is a long distance for Whitefoot. And so that journey was to him very long indeed. Of course, it seemed longer because of the constant frights which came one right after another. It really was a terrible journey. Yet if he had only known it, there wasn't a thing along the whole way to be afraid of. You know it often happens that people are frightened more by what they don't know than by what they do know.

XVI.
Whitefoot Climbs a Tree

I'd rather be frightened
With no cause for fear
Than fearful of nothing
When danger is near.
Whitefoot.

WHITEFOOT kept on going and going. Every time he thought that he was so tired he must stop, he would think of Shadow the Weasel and then go on again. By and by he became so tired that not even the thought of Shadow the Weasel could make him go much farther. So he began to look about for a safe hiding-place in which to rest.

Now the home which he had left had been a snug little room beneath the roots of a certain old stump. There he had lived for a long time in the greatest comfort. Little tunnels led to his storehouses and up to the surface of the snow. It had been a splendid place and one in which he had felt perfectly safe until Shadow the Weasel had appeared. Had you seen him playing about there, you would have thought him one of the little people of the ground, like his cousin Danny Meadow Mouse.

42

But Whitefoot is quite as much at home in trees as on the ground. In fact, he is quite as much at home in trees as is Chatterer the Red Squirrel, and a lot more at home in trees than is Striped Chipmunk, although Striped Chipmunk belongs to the Squirrel family. So now that he must find a hiding-place, Whitefoot decided that he would feel much safer in a tree than on the ground.

"If only I can find a hollow tree," whimpered Whitefoot. "I will feel ever so much safer in a tree than hiding in or near the ground in a strange place."

So Whitefoot began to look for a dead tree. You see, he knew that there was more likely to be a hollow in a dead tree than in a living tree. By and by he came to a tall, dead tree. He knew it was a dead tree, because there was no bark on it. But, of course, he couldn't tell whether or not that tree was hollow. I mean he couldn't tell from the ground.

"Oh, dear!" he whimpered again. "Oh, dear! I suppose I will have to climb this, and I am so tired. It ought to be hollow. There ought to be splendid holes in it. It is just the kind of a tree that Drummer the Woodpecker likes to make his house in. I shall be terribly disappointed if I don't find one of his houses somewhere in it, but I wish I hadn't got to climb it to find out. Well, here goes."

He looked anxiously this way. He looked anxiously that way. He looked anxiously the other way.

In fact, he looked anxiously every way. But he saw no one and nothing to be afraid of, and so he started up the tree.

He was half-way up when, glancing down, he saw a shadow moving across the snow. Once more Whitefoot's heart seemed to jump right up in his throat. That shadow was the shadow of someone flying. There couldn't be the least bit of doubt about it. Whitefoot flattened himself against the side of the tree and peeked around it. He was just in time to see a gray and black and white bird almost the size of Sammy Jay alight in the very next tree. He had come along near the ground and then risen sharply into the tree. His bill was black, and there was just a tiny hook on the end of it. Whitefoot knew who it was. It was Butcher the Shrike. Whitefoot shivered.

XVII.
Whitefoot Finds a Hole Just in Time

Just in time, not just too late,
Will make you master of your fate.
Whitefoot.

WHITEFOOT, half-way up that dead tree, flat-tened himself against the trunk and, with his heart going pit-a-pat, pit-a-pat with fright, peered around the tree at an enemy he had not seen for so long that he had quite forgotten there was such a one. It was Butcher the Shrike. Often he is called just Butcher Bird.

He did not look at all terrible. He was not quite as big as Sammy Jay. He had no terrible claws like the Hawks and Owls. There was a tiny hook at the end of his black bill, but it wasn't big enough to look very dreadful. But you cannot always judge a person by looks, and Whitefoot knew that Butcher was one to be feared.

So his heart went pit-a-pat, pit-a-pat as he won-dered if Butcher had seen him. He didn't have to wait long to find out. Butcher flew to a tree back of Whitefoot and then straight at him. Whitefoot dodged around to the other side of the tree. Then began a dreadful game. At least, it was dreadful to

45

Then began a dreadful game.
At least, it was dreadful to Whitefoot. *See page 45.*

Whitefoot. This way and that way around the trunk of that tree he dodged, while Butcher did his best to catch him.

Whitefoot would not have minded this so much, had he not been so tired, and had he known of a hiding-place close at hand. But he *was* tired, very tired, for you remember he had had what was a very long and terrible journey to him. He had felt almost too tired to climb that tree in the first place to see if it had any holes in it higher up. Now he didn't know whether to keep on going up or to go down. Two or three times he dodged around the tree without doing either. Then he decided to go up.

Now Butcher was enjoying this game of dodge. If he should catch Whitefoot, he would have a good dinner. If he didn't catch Whitefoot, he would simply go hungry a little longer. So you see, there was a very big difference in the feelings of Whitefoot and Butcher. Whitefoot had his life to lose, while Butcher had only a dinner to lose.

Dodging this way and dodging that way, White-foot climbed higher and higher. Twice he whisked around that tree trunk barely in time. All the time he was growing more and more tired, and more and more discouraged. Supposing he should find no hole in that tree!

"There must be one. There must be one," he kept saying over and over to himself, to keep his courage up. "I can't keep dodging much longer. If I don't find a hole pretty soon, Butcher will surely catch me. Oh, dear! Oh, dear!"

Just above Whitefoot was a broken branch. Only the stub of it remained. The next time he dodged around the trunk he found himself just below that stub. Oh, joy! There, close under that stub, was a round hole. Whitefoot didn't hesitate a second. He didn't wait to find out whether or not anyone was in that hole. He didn't even think that there might be someone in there. With a tiny little squeak of relief he darted in.

He was just in time. He was just in the nick of time. Butcher struck at him and just missed him as he disappeared in that hole. Whitefoot had saved his life and Butcher had missed a dinner.

XVIII.
An Unpleasant Surprise

Be careful never to be rude
Enough to thoughtlessly intrude.
Whitefoot.

IF ever anybody in the Great World felt relief and thankfulness, it was Whitefoot when he dodged into that hole in the dead tree just as Butcher the Shrike all but caught him. For a few minutes he did nothing but pant, for he was quite out of breath.

"I was right," he said over and over to himself, "I was right. I was sure there must be a hole in this tree. It is one of the old houses of Drummer the Woodpecker. Now I am safe."

Presently he peeped out. He wanted to see if Butcher was watching outside. He was just in time to see Butcher's gray and black and white coat disappearing among the trees. Butcher was not foolish enough to waste time watching for Whitefoot to come out. Whitefoot sighed happily. For the first time since he had started on his dreadful journey he felt safe. Nothing else mattered. He was hungry, but he didn't mind that. He was willing to go hungry for the sake of being safe.

Whitefoot watched until Butcher was out of

sight. Then he turned to see what that house was like. Right away he discovered that there was a soft, warm bed in it. It was made of leaves, grass, moss, and the lining of bark. It was a very fine bed indeed.

"My, my, my, but I am lucky," said Whitefoot to himself. "I wonder who could have made this fine bed. I certainly shall sleep comfortably here. Goodness knows, I need a rest. If I can find food enough near here, I'll make this my home. I couldn't ask for a better one."

Chuckling happily, Whitefoot began to pull away the top of that bed so as to get to the middle of it. And then he got a surprise. It was an unpleasant surprise. It was a most unpleasant surprise. There was someone in that bed! Yes, sir, there was someone curled up in a little round ball in the middle of that fine bed. It was someone with a coat of the softest, finest fur. Can you guess who it was? It was Timmy the Flying Squirrel.

It seemed to Whitefoot as if his heart flopped right over. You see at first he didn't recognize Timmy. Whitefoot is himself so very timid that his thought was to run; to get out of there as quickly as possible. But he had no place to run to, so he hesitated. Never in all his life had Whitefoot had a greater disappointment. He knew now that this splendid house was not for him.

Timmy the Flying Squirrel didn't move. He remained curled up in a soft little ball. He was asleep. Whitefoot remembered that Timmy sleeps during the day and seldom comes out until the Black Shadows come creeping out from the Purple Hills at the close of day. Whitefoot felt easier in his mind then. Timmy was so sound asleep that he knew nothing of his visitor. And so Whitefoot felt safe in staying long enough to get rested. Then he would go out and hunt for another home.

So down in the middle of that soft, warm bed Timmy the Flying Squirrel, curled up in a little round ball with his flat tail wrapped around him, slept peacefully, and on top of that soft bed Whitefoot the Wood Mouse rested and wondered what he should do next. Not in all the Green Forest could two more timid little people be found than the two in that old home of Drummer the Woodpecker.

XIX.
Whitefoot Finds a Home at Last

True independence he has known
Whose home has been his very own.
Whitefoot.

CURLED up in his splendid warm bed, Timmy the Flying Squirrel slept peacefully. He didn't know he had a visitor. He didn't know that on top of that same bed lay Whitefoot the Wood Mouse. Whitefoot wasn't asleep. No, indeed! Whitefoot was too worried to sleep. He knew he couldn't stay in that fine house because it belonged to Timmy. He knew that as soon as Timmy awoke, he, Whitefoot, would have to get out. Where should he go? He wished he knew. How he did long for the old home he had left. But when he thought of that, he remembered Shadow the Weasel. It was better to be homeless than to feel that at any minute Shadow the Weasel might appear.

It was getting late in the afternoon. Before long, jolly, round, red Mr. Sun would go to bed behind the Purple Hills, and the Black Shadows would come creeping through the Green Forest. Then Timmy the Flying Squirrel would awake. "It won't do for me to be here then," said Whitefoot to himself. "I must find some other place before he wakes. If only I knew this part of the Green Forest I might know where to go. As it is, I shall have to go hunt for a new home and trust to luck. Did ever a poor little Mouse have so much trouble?"

After awhile Whitefoot felt rested and peeped out of the doorway. No enemy was to be seen anywhere. Whitefoot crept out and climbed a little higher up in the tree. Presently he found another hole. He peeped inside and listened long and carefully. He didn't intend to make the mistake of going into another house where someone might be living.

At last, sure that there was no one in there, he crept in. Then he made a discovery. There were beech nuts in there and there were seeds. It was a storehouse! Whitefoot knew at once that it must be Timmy's storehouse. Right away he realized how very, very hungry he was. Of course, he had no right to any of those seeds or nuts. Certainly not! That is, he wouldn't have had any right had he been a boy or girl. But it is the law of the Green Forest that whatever anyone finds he may help himself to if he can.

So Whitefoot began to fill his empty little stomach with some of those seeds. He ate and ate and ate and quite forgot all his troubles. Just as he felt that he hadn't room for another seed, ̣ he heard the sound of claws outside on the trunk of the tree. In a flash he knew that Timmy the Flying Squirrel was awake, and that it wouldn't do to be found in there by him. In a jiffy Whitefoot was outside. He was just in time. Timmy was almost up to the entrance.

"Hi, there!" cried Timmy. "What were you doing in my storehouse?"

"I—I—I was looking for a new home," stammered Whitefoot.

"You mean you were stealing some of my food," snapped Timmy suspiciously.

"I—I—I did take a few seeds because I was almost starved. But truly I was looking for a new home," replied Whitefoot.

"What was the matter with your old home?" demanded Timmy.

Then Whitefoot told Timmy all about how he had been obliged to leave his old home because of Shadow the Weasel, of the terrible journey he had had, and how he didn't know where to go or what to do. Timmy listened suspiciously at first, but soon he made up his mind that Whitefoot was telling the truth. The mere mention of Shadow the Weasel made him very sober.

He scratched his nose thoughtfully. "Over in that tall, dead stub you can see from here is an old home of mine," said he. "No one lives in it now. I guess you can live there until you can find a better home. But remember to keep away from my storehouse."

So it was that Whitefoot found a new home.

XX.
Whitefoot Makes Himself at Home

> Look not too much on that behind
> Lest to the future you be blind.
> *Whitefoot.*

WHITEFOOT didn't wait to be told twice of that empty house. He thanked Timmy and then scampered over to that stub as fast as his legs would take him. Up the stub he climbed, and near the top he found a little round hole. Timmy had said no one was living there now, and so Whitefoot didn't hesitate to pop inside.

There was even a bed in there. It was an old bed, but it was dry and soft. It was quite clear that no one had been in there for a long time. With a little sigh of pure happiness, Whitefoot curled up in that bed for the sleep he so much needed. His stomach was full, and once more he felt safe. The very fact that this was an old house in which no one had lived for a long time made it safer. Whitefoot knew that those who lived in that part of the Green Forest probably knew that no one lived in that old stub, and so no one was likely to visit it.

He was so tired that he slept all night. Whitefoot is one of those who sleeps when he feels sleepy, whether it be by day or night. He prefers the night to be out and about in, because he feels safer then, but he often comes out by day. So when he awoke in the early morning, he promptly went out for a look about and to get acquainted with his new surroundings.

Just a little way off was the tall, dead tree in which Timmy the Flying Squirrel had his home. Timmy was nowhere to be seen. You see, he had been out most of the night and had gone to bed to sleep through the day. Whitefoot thought longingly of the good things in Timmy's storehouse in that same tree, but decided that it would be wisest to keep away from there. So he scurried about to see what he could find for a breakfast. It didn't take him long to find some pine cones in which a few seeds were still clinging. These would do nicely. Whitefoot ate what he wanted and then carried some of them back to his new home in the tall stub.

Then he went to work to tear to pieces the old bed in there and make it over to suit himself. It was an old bed of Timmy the Flying Squirrel, for you know this was Timmy's old house.

Whitefoot soon had the bed made over to suit him. And when this was done he felt quite at home. Then he started out to explore all about within a short distance of the old stub. He wanted to know every hole and every possible hiding-place all around, for it is on such knowledge that his life depends.

When at last he returned home he was very well satisfied. "It is going to be a good place to live," said he to himself. "There are plenty of hiding-places and I am going to be able to find enough to eat. It will be very nice to have Timmy the Flying Squirrel for a neighbor. I am sure he and I will get along together very nicely. I don't believe Shadow the Weasel, even if he should come around here, would bother to climb up this old stub. He probably would expect to find me living down in the ground or close to it, anyway. I certainly am glad that I am such a good climber. Now if Buster Bear doesn't come along in the spring and pull this old stub over, I'll have as fine a home as anyone could ask for."

And then, because happily it is the way with the little people of the Green Forest and the Green Meadows, Whitefoot forgot all about his terrible journey and the dreadful time he had had in finding his new home.

XXI.
Whitefoot Envies Timmy

A useless thing is envy;
A foolish thing to boot.
Why should a Fox who has a bark
Want like an Owl to hoot?

WHITEFOOT was beginning to feel quite at home. He would have been wholly contented but for one thing,—he had no well-filled store-house. This meant that each day he must hunt for his food.

It wasn't that Whitefoot minded hunting for food. He would have done that anyway, even though he had had close at hand a storehouse with plenty in it. But he would have felt easier in his mind. He would have had the comfortable feeling that if the weather turned so bad that he could not easily get out and about, he would not have to go hungry.

But Whitefoot is a happy little fellow and wisely made the best of things. At first he came out very little by day. He knew that there were many sharp eyes watching for him, and that he was more likely to be seen in the light of day than when the Black Shadows had crept all through the Green Forest.

He would peek out of his doorway and watch for chance visitors in the daytime. Twice he saw Butcher the Shrike alight a short distance from the tree in which Timmy lived. He knew Butcher had not forgotten that he had chased a badly frightened Mouse into a hole in that tree. Once he saw Whitey the Snowy Owl and so knew that Whitey had not yet returned to the Far North. Once Reddy Fox trotted along right past the foot of the old stub in which Whitefoot lived, and didn't even suspect that he was anywhere near. Twice he saw Old Man Coyote trotting past, and once Terror the Goshawk alighted on that very stub, and sat there for half an hour.

So Whitefoot formed the habit of doing just what Timmy the Flying Squirrel did; he remained in his house for most of the day and came out when the Black Shadows began to creep in among the trees. Timmy came out about the same time, and they had become the best of friends.

Now Whitefoot is not much given to envying others, but as night after night he watched Timmy a little envy crept into his heart in spite of all he could do. Timmy would nimbly climb to the top of a tree and then jump. Down he would come in a long beautiful glide, for all the world as if he were sliding on the air.

The first time Whitefoot saw him do it he held his breath. He really didn't know what to make of it. The nearest tree to the one from which Timmy had jumped was so far away that it didn't seem possible anyone without wings could reach it without first going to the ground.

"Oh!" squeaked Whitefoot. "Oh! He'll kill himself! He surely will kill himself! He'll break his neck!" But Timmy did nothing of the kind. He sailed down, down, down and alighted on that distant tree a foot or two from the bottom; and without stopping a second scampered up to the top of that tree and once more jumped. Whitefoot had hard work to believe his own eyes. Timmy seemed to be jumping just for the pleasure of it. As a matter of fact, he was. He was getting his evening exercise.

Whitefoot sighed. "I wish I could jump like that," said he to himself. "I wouldn't ever be afraid of anybody if I could jump like that. I envy Timmy. I do so."

XXII.
Timmy Proves To Be a True Neighbor

He proves himself a neighbor true
Who seeks a kindly deed to do.
Whitefoot.

OCCASIONALLY Timmy the Flying Squirrel came over to visit Whitefoot. If Whitefoot was in his house he always knew when Timmy arrived. He would hear a soft thump down near the bottom of the tall stub. He would know instantly that thump was made by Timmy striking the foot of the stub after a long jump from the top of a tree. Whitefoot would poke his head out of his doorway and there, sure enough, would be Timmy scrambling up towards him.

Whitefoot had grown to admire Timmy with all his might. It seemed to him that Timmy was the most wonderful of all the people he knew. You see there was none of the others who could jump as Timmy could. Timmy on his part enjoyed having Whitefoot for a neighbor. Few of the little people of the Green Forest are more timid than Timmy the Flying Squirrel, but here was one beside whom Timmy actually felt bold. It was such a new feeling that Timmy enjoyed it.

So it was that in the dusk of early evening, just after the Black Shadows had come creeping out from the Purple Hills across the Green Meadows and through the Green Forest, these two little neighbors would start out to hunt for food. Whitefoot never went far from the tall, dead stub in which he was now living. He didn't dare to. He wanted to be where at the first sign of danger he could scamper back there to safety. Timmy would go some distance, but he was seldom gone long. He liked to be where he could watch and talk with Whitefoot. You see Timmy is very much like other people,—he likes to gossip a little.

One evening Whitefoot had found it hard work to find enough food to fill his stomach. He had kept going a little farther and a little farther from home. Finally he was farther from it than he had ever been before. Timmy had filled his stomach and from near the top of a tree was watching White-foot. Suddenly what seemed like a great Black Shadow floated right over the tree in which Timmy was sitting, and stopped on the top of a tall, dead tree. It was Hooty the Owl, and it was simply good fortune that Timmy happened to see him. Timmy did not move. He knew that he was safe so long as he kept perfectly still. He knew that Hooty didn't know he was there. Unless he moved, those great eyes of Hooty's, wonderful as they were, would not see him.

Timmy looked over to where he had last seen

Whitefoot. There he was picking out seeds from a pine cone on the ground. The trunk of a tree was between him and Hooty. But Timmy knew that Whitefoot hadn't seen Hooty, and that any minute he might run out from behind that tree. If he did Hooty would see him, and silently as a shadow would swoop down and catch him. What was to be done?

"It's no business of mine," said Timmy to himself. "Whitefoot must look out for himself. It is no business of mine at all. Perhaps Hooty will fly away before Whitefoot moves. I don't want anything to happen to Whitefoot, but if something does, it will be his own fault; he should keep better watch."

For a few minutes nothing happened. Then Whitefoot finished the last seed in that cone and started to look for more. Timmy knew that in a moment Hooty would see Whitefoot. What do you think Timmy did? He jumped. Yes, sir, he jumped. Down, down, down, straight past the tree on which sat Hooty the Owl, Timmy sailed. Hooty saw him. Of course. He couldn't help but see him. He spread his great wings and was after Timmy in an instant. Timmy struck near the foot of a tree and without wasting a second darted around to the other side. He was just in time. Hooty was already reaching for him. Up the tree ran Timmy and jumped again. Again Hooty was too late. And so Timmy led Hooty the Owl away from Whitefoot the Wood Mouse.

XXIII.
Whitefoot Spends a Dreadful Night

Pity those who suffer fright
In the dark and stilly night.
Whitefoot.

ONE night of his life Whitefoot will never forget so long as he lives. Even now it makes him shiver just to think of it. Yes, sir, he shivers even now whenever he thinks of that night. The Black Shadows had come early that evening, so that it was quite dusk when Whitefoot crept out of his snug little bed and climbed up to the round hole which was the doorway of his home. He had just poked his nose out that little round doorway when there was the most terrible sound. It seemed to him as if it was in his very ears, so loud and terrible was it. It frightened him so that he simply let go and tumbled backward down inside his house. Of course it didn't hurt him any, for he landed on his soft bed.

"Whooo-hoo-hoo, whooo-hoo!" came that terrible sound again, and Whitefoot shook until his little teeth rattled. At least, that is the way it seemed to him. It was the voice of Hooty the Owl, and Whitefoot knew that Hooty was sitting on the top of that very stub. He was, so to speak, on the roof of Whitefoot's house.

Now in all the Green Forest there is no sound that strikes terror to the hearts of the little people of feathers and fur equal to the hunting call of Hooty the Owl. Hooty knows this. No one knows it better than he does. That is why he uses it. He knows that many of the little people are asleep, safely hidden away. He knows that it would be quite useless for him to simply look for them. He would starve before he could find a dinner in that way. But he knows that anyone wakened from sleep in great fright is sure to move, and if they do this they are almost equally sure to make some little sound. His ears are so wonderful that they can catch the faintest sound and tell exactly where it comes from. So he uses that terrible hunting cry to frighten the little people and make them move.

Now Whitefoot knew that he was safe. Hooty couldn't possibly get at him, even should he find out that he was in there. There was nothing to fear, but just the same, Whitefoot shivered and shook and jumped almost out of his skin every time that Hooty hooted. He just couldn't help it.

"He can't get me. I know he can't get me. I'm perfectly safe. I'm just as safe as if he were miles away. There's nothing to be afraid of. It is silly to be afraid. Probably Hooty doesn't even know I am inside here. Even if he does, it doesn't really matter." Whitefoot said these things to himself over and over again. Then Hooty would send out that fierce, terrible hunting call and Whitefoot would jump and shake just as before.

After awhile all was still. Gradually Whitefoot stopped trembling. He guessed that Hooty had flown away. Still he remained right where he was for a very long time. He didn't intend to foolishly take any chances. So he waited and waited and waited.

At last he was sure that Hooty had left. Once more he climbed up to his little round doorway and there he waited some time before poking even his nose outside. Then, just as he had made up his mind to go out, that terrible sound rang out again, and just as before he tumbled heels over head down on his bed.

Whitefoot didn't go out that night at all. It was a moonlight night and just the kind of a night to be out. Instead Whitefoot lay in his little bed and shivered and shook, for all through that long night every once in a while Hooty the Owl would hoot from the top of that stub.

XXIV.
Whitefoot the Wood Mouse Is Unhappy

Unhappiness without a cause you never, never find;
It may be in the stomach, or it may be in the mind.
                                                    Whitefoot.

WHITEFOOT THE WOOD MOUSE should have
been happy, but he wasn't. Winter had gone
and sweet Mistress Spring had brought joy to all
the Green Forest. Everyone was happy, Whitefoot
no less so than his neighbors at first. Up from the
Sunny South came the feathered friends and at
once began planning new homes. Twitterings and
songs filled the air. Joy was everywhere. Food
became plentiful, and Whitefoot became sleek and
fat. That is, he became as fat as a lively Wood
Mouse ever does become. None of his enemies had
discovered his new home, and he had little to
worry about.

But by and by Whitefoot began to feel less joyous. Day by day he grew more and more unhappy.
He no longer took pleasure in his fine home. He
began to wander about for no particular reason.
He wandered much farther from home than he had
ever been in the habit of doing. At times he would

sit and listen, but what he was listening for he didn't know.

"There is something the matter with me, and I don't know what it is," said Whitefoot to himself forlornly. "It can't be anything I have eaten. I have nothing to worry about. Yet there is something wrong with me. I'm losing my appetite. Nothing tastes good anymore. I want something, but I don't know what it is I want."

He tried to tell his troubles to his nearest neighbor, Timmy the Flying Squirrel, but Timmy was too busy to listen. When Peter Rabbit happened along, Whitefoot tried to tell him. But Peter himself was too happy and too eager to learn all the news in the Green Forest to listen. No one had any interest in Whitefoot's troubles. Everyone was too busy with his own affairs.

So day by day Whitefoot the Wood Mouse grew more and more unhappy, and when the dusk of early evening came creeping through the Green Forest, he sat about and moped instead of running about and playing as he had been in the habit of doing. The beautiful song of Melody the Wood Thrush somehow filled him with sadness instead of with the joy he had always felt before. The very happiness of those about him seemed to make him more unhappy.

Once he almost decided to go hunt for another home, but somehow he couldn't get interested even in this. He did start out, but he had not gone far before he had forgotten all about what he had started for. Always he had loved to run about and climb and jump for the pure pleasure of it, but now he no longer did these things. He was unhappy, was Whitefoot. Yes, sir, he was unhappy; and for no cause at all so far as he could see.

XXV.
Whitefoot Finds Out What the Matter Was

Pity the lonely, for deep in the heart
Is an ache that no doctor can heal by his art.
                                        Whitefoot.

O F all the little people of the Green Forest
Whitefoot seemed to be the only one who was
unhappy. And because he didn't know why he felt
so he became day by day more unhappy. Perhaps I
should say that night by night he became more
unhappy, for during the brightness of the day he
slept most of the time.

"There is something wrong, something wrong,"
he would say over and over to himself.

"It must be with me, because everybody else is
happy, and this is the happiest time of all the year.
I wish someone would tell me what ails me. I want
to be happy, but somehow I just can't be."

One evening he wandered a little farther from
home than usual. He wasn't going anywhere in particular. He had nothing in particular to do. He was
just wandering about because somehow he
couldn't remain at home. Not far away Melody the
Wood Thrush was pouring out his beautiful

evening song. Whitefoot stopped to listen. Somehow it made him more unhappy than ever. Melody stopped singing for a few moments. It was just then that Whitefoot heard a faint sound. It was a gentle drumming. Whitefoot pricked up his ears and listened. There it was again. He knew instantly how that sound was made. It was made by dainty little feet beating very fast on an old log. Whitefoot had drummed that way himself many times. It was soft, but clear, and it lasted only a moment.

Right then something very strange happened to Whitefoot. Yes, sir, something very strange happened to Whitefoot. All in a flash he felt better. At first he didn't know why. He just did, that was all. Without thinking what he was doing, he began to drum himself. Then he listened. At first he heard nothing. Then, soft and low, came that drumming sound again. Whitefoot replied to it. All the time he kept feeling better. He ran a little nearer to the place from which that drumming sound had come and then once more drummed. At first he got no reply.

Then in a few minutes he heard it again, only this time it came from a different place. Whitefoot became quite excited. He knew that that drumming was done by another Wood Mouse, and all in a flash it came over him what had been the matter with him.

"I have been lonely!" exclaimed Whitefoot. "That is all that has been the trouble with me. I have been lonely and didn't know it. I wonder if that other Wood Mouse has felt the same way."

Again he drummed and again came that soft reply. Once more Whitefoot hurried in the direction of it, and once more he was disappointed when the next reply came from a different place. By now he was getting quite excited. He was bound to find that other Wood Mouse. Every time he heard that drumming, funny little thrills ran all over him. He didn't know why. They just did, that was all. He simply *must* find that other Wood Mouse. He forgot everything else. He didn't even notice where he was going. He would drum, then wait for a reply. As soon as he heard it, he would scamper in the direction of it, and then pause to drum again. Sometimes the reply would be very near, then again it would be so far away that a great fear would fill Whitefoot's heart that the stranger was running away.

XXVI.
Love Fills the Heart of Whitefoot

Joyous all the winds that blow
To the heart with love aglow.
Whitefoot.

IT was a wonderful game of hide-and-seek that
Whitefoot the Wood Mouse was playing in the
dusk of early evening. Whitefoot was "it" all the
time. That is, he was the one who had to do all the
hunting. Just who he was hunting for he didn't
know. He knew it was another Wood Mouse, but it
was a stranger, and do what he would, he couldn't
get so much as a glimpse of this little stranger. He
would drum with his feet and after a slight pause
there would be an answering drum. Then Whitefoot would run as fast as he could in that direction
only to find no one at all. Then he would drum
again and the reply would come from another
direction.

Every moment Whitefoot became more excited.
He forgot everything, even danger, in his desire to
see that little drummer. Once or twice he actually
lost his temper in his disappointment. But this was
only for a moment. He was too eager to find that little drummer to be angry very long.

At last there came a time when there was no reply to his drumming. He drummed and listened, then drummed again and listened. Nothing was to be heard. There was no reply. Whitefoot's heart sank.

All the old lonesomeness crept over him again. He didn't know which way to turn to look for that stranger. When he had drummed until he was tired, he sat on the end of an old log, a perfect picture of disappointment. He was so disappointed that he could have cried if it would have done any good.

Just as he had about made up his mind that there was nothing to do but to try to find his way home, his keen little ears caught the faintest rustle of dry leaves. Instantly Whitefoot was alert and watchful. Long ago he had learned to be suspicious of rustling leaves. They might have been rustled by the feet of an enemy stealing up on him. No Wood Mouse who wants to live long is ever heedless of rustling leaves. As still as if he couldn't move, Whitefoot sat staring at the place from which that faint sound had seemed to come. For two or three minutes he heard and saw nothing. Then another leaf rustled a little bit to one side. Whitefoot turned like a flash, his feet gathered under him ready for a long jump for safety.

At first he saw nothing. Then he became aware of two bright, soft little eyes watching him. He stared at them very hard and then all over him crept those funny thrills he had felt when he had first heard the drumming of the stranger. He knew without being told that those eyes belonged to the little drummer with whom he had been playing hide and seek so long.

Whitefoot held his breath, he was so afraid that those eyes would vanish. Finally he rather timidly jumped down from the log and started toward those two soft eyes. They vanished. Whitefoot's heart sank. He was tempted to rush forward, but he didn't. He sat still. There was a slight rustle off to the right. A little ray of moonlight made its way down through the branches of the trees just there, and in the middle of the light spot it made sat a timid little person. It seemed to Whitefoot that he was looking at the most beautiful Wood Mouse in all the Great World. Suddenly he felt very shy and timid himself.

"Who—who—who are you?" he stammered.

"I am little Miss Dainty," replied the stranger bashfully.

Right then and there Whitefoot's heart was filled so full of something that it seemed as if it would burst. It was love. All in that instant he knew that he had found the most wonderful thing in all the Great World, which of course is love. He knew that he just couldn't live without little Miss Dainty.

"I am little Miss Dainty," replied the stranger bashfully.
See page 75.

XXVII.
Mr. and Mrs. Whitefoot

When all is said and all is done
'Tis only love of two makes one.
Whitefoot.

LITTLE Miss Dainty, the most beautiful and wonderful Wood Mouse in all the Great World, according to Whitefoot, was very shy and very timid. It took Whitefoot a long time to make her believe that he really couldn't live without her. At least, she pretended not to believe it. If the truth were known, little Miss Dainty felt just the same way about Whitefoot. But Whitefoot didn't know this, and I am afraid she teased him a great deal before she told him that she loved him just as he loved her.

But at last little Miss Dainty shyly admitted that she loved Whitefoot just as much as he loved her and was willing to become Mrs. Whitefoot. Secretly she thought Whitefoot the most wonderful Wood Mouse in the Great World, but she didn't tell him so. The truth is, she made him feel as if she were doing him a great favor.

As for Whitefoot, he was so happy that he actually tried to sing. Yes, sir, Whitefoot tried to sing,

and he really did very well for a Mouse. He was
ready and eager to do anything that Mrs. Whitefoot
wanted to do. Together they scampered about in
the moonlight, hunting for good things to eat, and
poking their inquisitive little noses into every little
place they could find. Whitefoot forgot that he had
ever been sad and lonely. He raced about and did
all sorts of funny things from pure joy, but he never
once forgot to watch out for danger. In fact he was
more watchful than ever, for now he was watching
for Mrs. Whitefoot as well as for himself.

At last Whitefoot rather timidly suggested that
they should go see his fine home in a certain hollow stub. Mrs. Whitefoot insisted that they should
go to her home. Whitefoot agreed on condition
that she would afterwards visit his home. So
together they went back to Mrs. Whitefoot's home.
Whitefoot pretended that he liked it very much,
but in his heart he thought his own home was very
much better, and he felt quite sure that Mrs. Whitefoot would agree with him once she had seen it.

But Mrs. Whitefoot was very well satisfied with
her old home and not at all anxious to leave it. It
was in an old hollow stump close to the ground. It
was just such a place as Shadow the Weasel would
be sure to visit should he happen along that way. It
didn't seem at all safe to Whitefoot. In fact it worried him. Then, too, it was not in such a pleasant
place as was his own home. Of course he didn't say
this, but pretended to admire everything.

Two days and nights they spent there. Then Whitefoot suggested that they should visit his home. "Of course, my dear, we will not have to live there unless you want to, but I want you to see it," said he.

Mrs. Whitefoot didn't appear at all anxious to go. She began to make excuses for staying right where they were. You see, she had a great love for that old home. They were sitting just outside the doorway talking about the matter when Whitefoot caught a glimpse of a swiftly moving form not far off. It was Shadow the Weasel. Neither of them breathed. Shadow passed without looking in their direction. When he was out of sight, Mrs. Whitefoot shivered.

"Let's go over to your home right away," she whispered. "I've never seen Shadow about here before, but now that he has been here once, he may come again."

"We'll start at once," replied Whitefoot, and for once he was glad that Shadow the Weasel was about.

XXVIII.
Mrs. Whitefoot Decides on a Home

When Mrs. Mouse makes up her mind
Then Mr. Mouse best get behind.
Whitefoot.

WHITEFOOT THE WOOD MOUSE was very proud of his home. He showed it as he led Mrs. Whitefoot there. He felt sure that she would say at once that that would be the place for them to live. You remember that it was high up in a tall, dead stub and had once been the home of Timmy the Flying Squirrel.

"There, my dear, what do you think of that?" said Whitefoot proudly as they reached the little round doorway.

Mrs. Whitefoot said nothing, but at once went inside. She was gone what seemed a long time to Whitefoot, anxiously waiting outside. You see, Mrs. Whitefoot is a very thorough small person, and she was examining the inside of that house from top to bottom. At last she appeared at the doorway.

"Don't you think this is a splendid house?" asked Whitefoot rather timidly.

"It is very good of its kind," replied Mrs. Whitefoot.

Whitefoot's heart sank. He didn't like the tone in which Mrs. Whitefoot had said that.

"Just what do you mean, my dear?" Whitefoot asked.

"I mean," replied Mrs. Whitefoot, in a most decided way, "that it is a very good house for winter, but it won't do at all for summer. That is, it won't do for me. In the first place it is so high up that if we should have babies, I would worry all the time for fear the darlings would have a bad fall. Besides, I don't like an inside house for summer. I think, Whitefoot, we must look around and find a new home."

As she spoke Mrs. Whitefoot was already starting down the stub. Whitefoot followed.

"All right, my dear, all right," said he meekly. "You know best. This seems to me like a very fine home, but of course, if you don't like it we'll look for another."

Mrs. Whitefoot said nothing, but led the way down the tree with Whitefoot meekly following. Then began a patient search all about. Mrs. Whitefoot appeared to know just what she wanted and turned up her nose at several places Whitefoot thought would make fine homes. She hardly glanced at a fine hollow log Whitefoot found. She merely poked her nose in at a splendid hole beneath the roots of an old stump. Whitefoot began to grow tired from running about and climbing stumps and trees and bushes.

He stopped to rest and lost sight of Mrs. White-foot. A moment later he heard her calling excited-ly. When he found her, she was up in a small tree, sitting on the edge of an old nest a few feet above the ground. It was a nest that had once belonged to Melody the Wood Thrush. Mrs. Whitefoot was sit-ting on the edge of it, and her bright eyes snapped with excitement and pleasure.

"I've found it!" she cried. "I've found it! It is just what I have been looking for."

"Found what?" Whitefoot asked. "I don't see any-thing but an old nest of Melody's."

"I've found the home we've been looking for, stu-pid," retorted Mrs. Whitefoot.

Still Whitefoot stared. "I don't see any house," said he.

Mrs. Whitefoot stamped her feet impatiently. "Right here, stupid," said she. "This old nest will make us the finest and safest home that ever was. No one will ever think of looking for us here. We must get busy at once and fix it up."

Even then Whitefoot didn't understand. Always he had lived either in a hole in the ground, or in a hollow stump or tree. How they were to live in that old nest he couldn't see at all.

XXIX.
Making Over an Old House

A home is always what you make it.
With love there you will ne'er forsake it.
                                        Whitefoot.

WHITEFOOT climbed up to the old nest of Melody the Wood Thrush over the edge of which little Mrs. Whitefoot was looking down at him. It took Whitefoot hardly a moment to get up there, for the nest was only a few feet above the ground in a young tree, and you know Whitefoot is a very good climber.

He found Mrs. Whitefoot very much excited. She was delighted with that old nest and she showed it. For his part, Whitefoot couldn't see anything but a deserted old house of no use to anyone. To be sure, it had been a very good home in its time. It had been made of tiny twigs, stalks of old weeds, leaves, little fine roots and mud. It was still quite solid, and was firmly fixed in a crotch of the young tree. But Whitefoot couldn't see how it could be turned into a home for a Mouse. He said as much.

Little Mrs. Whitefoot became more excited than ever. "You dear old stupid," said she, "whatever is the matter with you? Don't you see that all we need

83

do is to put a roof on, make an entrance on the under side, and make a soft comfortable bed inside to make it a delightful home?"

"I don't see why we don't make a new home altogether," protested Whitefoot. "It seems to me that hollow stub of mine is ever so much better than this. That has good solid walls, and we won't have to do a thing to it."

"I told you once before that it doesn't suit me for summer," replied little Mrs. Whitefoot rather sharply, because she was beginning to lose patience. "It will be all right for winter, but winter is a long way off. It may suit you for summer, but it doesn't suit me, and this place does. So this is where we are going to live."

"Certainly, my dear. Certainly," replied Whitefoot very meekly. "If you want to live here, here we will live. But I must confess it isn't clear to me yet how we are going to make a decent home out of this old nest."

"Don't you worry about that," replied Mrs. Whitefoot. "You can get the material, and I'll attend to the rest. Let us waste no time about it. I am anxious to get our home finished and to feel a little bit settled. I have already planned just what has got to be done and how we will do it. Now you go look for some nice soft, dry weed stalks and strips of soft bark, and moss and any other soft, tough material that you can find. Just get busy and don't stop to talk."

Of course Whitefoot did as he was told. He ran down to the ground and began to hunt for the things Mrs. Whitefoot wanted. He was very particular about it. He still didn't think much of her idea of making over that old home of Melody's, but if she *would* do it, he meant that she should have the very best of materials to do it with.

So back and forth from the ground to the old nest in the tree Whitefoot hurried, and presently there was quite a pile of weed stalks and soft grass and strips of bark in the old nest. Mrs. Whitefoot joined Whitefoot in hunting for just the right things, but she spent more time in arranging the material. Over that old nest she made a fine high roof. Down through the lower side she cut a little round doorway just big enough for them to pass through. Unless you happened to be underneath looking up, you never would have guessed there was an entrance at all. Inside was a snug, round room, and in this she made the softest and most comfortable of beds. As it began to look more and more like a home, Whitefoot himself became as excited and eager as Mrs. Whitefoot had been from the beginning. "It certainly is going to be a fine home," said Whitefoot.

"Didn't I tell you it would be?" retorted Mrs. Whitefoot.

XXX.
The Whitefoots Enjoy Their New Home

No home is ever mean or poor
Where love awaits you at the door.
                                        Whitefoot.

"THERE," said Mrs. Whitefoot, as she worked a strip of white birch bark into the roof of the new home she and Whitefoot had been building out of the old home of Melody the Wood Thrush, "this finishes the roof. I don't think any water will get through it even in the hardest rain."

"It is wonderful," declared Whitefoot admiringly. "Wherever did you learn to build such a house as this?"

"From my mother," replied Mrs. Whitefoot. "I was born in just such a home. It makes the finest kind of a home for Wood Mouse babies."

"You don't think there is danger that the wind will blow it down, do you?" ventured Whitefoot.

"Of course I don't," retorted little Mrs. Whitefoot scornfully. "Hasn't this old nest remained right where it is for over a year? Do you suppose that if I had thought there was the least bit of danger that it would blow down, I would have used it? Do credit me with a little sense, my dear."

"Yes'm, I do," replied Whitefoot meekly. "You are the most sensible person in all the Great World. I wasn't finding fault. You see, I have always lived in a hole in the ground or a hollow stump, or a hole in a tree, and I have not yet become used to a home that moves about and rocks as this one does when the wind blows. But if you say it is all right, why of course it is all right. Probably I will get used to it after awhile."

Whitefoot did get used to it. After living in it for a few days, it no longer seemed strange, and he no longer minded its swaying when the wind blew. The fact is, he rather enjoyed it. So Whitefoot and Mrs. Whitefoot settled down to enjoy their new home. Now and then they added a bit to it here and there.

Somehow Whitefoot felt unusually safe, safer than he had ever felt in any of his other homes. You see, he had seen several feathered folk alight close to it and not give it a second look. He knew that they had seen that home, but had mistaken it for what it had once been, the deserted home of one of their own number.

Whitefoot had chuckled. He had chuckled long and heartily. "If they make that mistake," said he to himself, "everybody else is likely to make it. That home of ours is right in plain sight, yet I do believe it is safer than the best hidden home I ever had before. Shadow the Weasel never will think of climbing up this little tree to look at an old nest, and Shadow is the one I am most afraid of."

It was only a day or two later that Buster Bear happened along that way. Now Buster is very fond of tender Wood Mouse. More than once Whitefoot had had a narrow escape from Buster's big claws as they tore open an old stump or dug into the ground after him. He saw Buster glance up at the new home without the slightest interest in those shrewd little eyes of his. Then Buster shuffled on to roll over an old log and lick up the ants he found under it. Again Whitefoot chuckled. "Yes, sir," said he. "It is the safest home I've ever had."

So Whitefoot and little Mrs. Whitefoot were very happy in the home which they had built, and for once in his life Whitefoot did very little worrying. Life seemed more beautiful than it had ever been before. And he almost forgot that there was such a thing as a hungry enemy.

XXXI.
Whitefoot Is Hurt

The hurts that hardest are to bear
Come from those for whom we care.
Whitefoot.

WHITEFOOT was hurt. Yes, sir, Whitefoot was hurt. He was very much hurt. It wasn't a bodily hurt; it was an inside hurt. It was a hurt that made his heart ache. And to make it worse, he couldn't understand it at all. One evening he had been met at the little round doorway by little Mrs. Whitefoot.

"You can't come in," said she.

"Why can't I?" demanded Whitefoot, in the greatest surprise.

"Never mind why. You can't, and that is all there is to it," replied Mrs. Whitefoot.

"You mean I can't ever come in anymore?" asked Whitefoot.

"I don't know about that," replied Mrs. Whitefoot, "but you can't come in now, nor for some time. I think the best thing you can do is to go back to your old home in the hollow stub."

Whitefoot stared at little Mrs. Whitefoot quite as if he thought she had gone crazy. Then he lost his temper. "I guess I'll come in if I want to," said he. "This home is quite as much my home as it is yours. You have no right to keep me out of it. Just you get out of my way."

But little Mrs. Whitefoot didn't get out of his way, and do what he would, Whitefoot couldn't get in. You see she quite filled that little round doorway. Finally, he had to give up trying. Three times he came back and each time he found little Mrs. Whitefoot in the doorway. And each time she drove him away. Finally, for lack of any other place to go to, he returned to his old home in the old stub. Once he had thought this the finest home possible, but now somehow it didn't suit him at all. The truth is he missed little Mrs. Whitefoot, and so what had once been a home was now only a place in which to hide and sleep.

Whitefoot's anger did not last long. It was replaced by that hurt feeling. He felt that he must have done something little Mrs. Whitefoot did not like, but though he thought and thought he couldn't remember a single thing. Several times he went back to see if Mrs. Whitefoot felt any differently, but found she didn't. Finally she told him rather sharply to go away and stay away. After that Whitefoot didn't venture over to the new home. He would sometimes sit a short distance away and gaze at it longingly. All the joy had gone out of the beautiful springtime for him. He was quite as unhappy as he had been before he met little Mrs.

Whitefoot. You see, he was even more lonely than he had been then. And added to this loneliness was that hurt feeling, which made it ever and ever so much worse. It was very hard to bear.

"If I could understand it, it wouldn't be so bad," he kept saying over and over again to himself, "but I don't understand it. I don't understand why Mrs. Whitefoot doesn't love me anymore."

XXXII.
The Surprise

Surprises sometimes are so great
You're tempted to believe in fate.
Whitefoot.

ONE never-to-be-forgotten evening Whitefoot met Mrs. Whitefoot and she invited him to come back to their home. Of course Whitefoot was delighted.

"Sh-h-h," said little Mrs. Whitefoot, as Whitefoot entered the snug little room of the house they had built in the old nest of Melody the Wood Thrush. Whitefoot hesitated. In the first place, it was dark in there. In the second place, he had the feeling that somehow that little bedroom seemed crowded. It hadn't been that way the last time he was there. Mrs. Whitefoot was right in front of him, and she seemed very much excited about something.

Presently she crowded to one side. "Come here and look," said she.

Whitefoot looked. In the middle of a soft bed of moss was a squirming mass of legs and funny little heads. At first that was all Whitefoot could make out.

"Don't you think this is the most wonderful sur-

prise that ever was?" whispered little Mrs. Whitefoot. "Aren't they darlings? Aren't you proud of
them?"

By this time Whitefoot had made out that that
squirming mass of legs and heads was composed
of baby Mice. He counted them. There were four.
"Whose are they, and what are they doing here?"
Whitefoot asked in a queer voice.

"Why, you old stupid, they are yours,—yours
and mine," declared little Mrs. Whitefoot. "Did you
ever, ever see such beautiful babies? Now I guess
you understand why I kept you away from here."

Whitefoot shook his head. "No," said he, "I don't
understand at all. I don't see yet what you drove
me away for."

"Why, you blessed old dear, there wasn't room
for you when those babies came; I had to have all
the room there was. It wouldn't have done to have
had you running in and out and disturbing them
when they were so tiny. I had to be alone with
them, and that is why I made you go off and live by
yourself. I am so proud of them, I don't know what
to do. Aren't you proud, Whitefoot? Aren't you the
proudest Wood Mouse in all the Green Forest?"

Of course Whitefoot should have promptly said
that he was, but the truth is, Whitefoot wasn't
proud at all. You see, he was so surprised that he
hadn't yet had time to feel that they were really
his. In fact, just then he felt a wee bit jealous of
them. It came over him that they would take all the

time and attention of little Mrs. Whitefoot. So Whitefoot didn't answer that question. He simply sat and stared at those four squirming babies.

Finally little Mrs. Whitefoot gently pushed him out and followed him. "Of course," said she, "there isn't room for you to stay here now. You will have to sleep in your old home because there isn't room in here for both of us and the babies too."

Whitefoot's heart sank. He had thought that he was to stay and that everything would be just as it had been before. "Can't I come over here any-more?" he asked rather timidly.

"What a foolish question!" cried little Mrs. White-foot. "Of course you can. You will have to help take care of these babies. Just as soon as they are big enough, you will have to help teach them how to hunt for food and how to watch out for danger, and all the things that a wise Wood Mouse knows. Why, they couldn't get along without you. Neither could I," she added softly.

At that Whitefoot felt better. And suddenly there was a queer swelling in his heart. It was the beginning of pride, pride in those wonderful babies.

"You have given me the best surprise that ever was, my dear," said Whitefoot softly. "Now I think I will go and look for some supper."

So now we will leave Whitefoot and his family. You see there are two very lively little people of the Green Forest who demand attention and insist on having it. They are Buster Bear's Twins, and this is to be the title of the next book.*

Buster Bear's Twins is available from Dover Publications (0-486-40790-X).

A CATALOG OF SELECTED

DOVER BOOKS

IN ALL FIELDS OF INTEREST

A CATALOG OF SELECTED DOVER
BOOKS IN ALL FIELDS OF INTEREST

CONCERNING THE SPIRITUAL IN ART, Wassily Kandinsky. Pioneering work by father of abstract art. Thoughts on color theory, nature of art. Analysis of earlier masters. 12 illustrations. 80pp. of text. 5⅜ x 8½. 0-486-23411-8

CELTIC ART: The Methods of Construction, George Bain. Simple geometric techniques for making Celtic interlacements, spirals, Kells-type initials, animals, humans, etc. Over 500 illustrations. 160pp. 9 x 12. (Available in U.S. only.) 0-486-22923-8

AN ATLAS OF ANATOMY FOR ARTISTS, Fritz Schider. Most thorough reference work on art anatomy in the world. Hundreds of illustrations, including selections from works by Vesalius, Leonardo, Goya, Ingres, Michelangelo, others. 593 illustrations. 192pp. 7⅞ x 10¼. 0-486-20241-0

CELTIC HAND STROKE-BY-STROKE (Irish Half-Uncial from "The Book of Kells"): An Arthur Baker Calligraphy Manual, Arthur Baker. Complete guide to creating each letter of the alphabet in distinctive Celtic manner. Covers hand position, strokes, pens, inks, paper, more. Illustrated. 48pp. 8¼ x 11. 0-486-24336-2

EASY ORIGAMI, John Montroll. Charming collection of 32 projects (hat, cup, pelican, piano, swan, many more) specially designed for the novice origami hobbyist. Clearly illustrated easy-to-follow instructions insure that even beginning papercrafters will achieve successful results. 48pp. 8¼ x 11. 0-486-27298-2

BLOOMINGDALE'S ILLUSTRATED 1886 CATALOG: Fashions, Dry Goods and Housewares, Bloomingdale Brothers. Famed merchants' extremely rare catalog depicting about 1,700 products: clothing, housewares, firearms, dry goods, jewelry, more. Invaluable for dating, identifying vintage items. Also, copyright-free graphics for artists, designers. Co-published with Henry Ford Museum & Greenfield Village. 160pp. 8¼ x 11. 0-486-25780-0

THE ART OF WORLDLY WISDOM, Baltasar Gracian. "Think with the few and speak with the many," "Friends are a second existence," and "Be able to forget" are among this 1637 volume's 300 pithy maxims. A perfect source of mental and spiritual refreshment, it can be opened at random and appreciated either in brief or at length. 128pp. 5⅜ x 8½. 0-486-44034-6

JOHNSON'S DICTIONARY: A Modern Selection, Samuel Johnson (E. L. McAdam and George Milne, eds.). This modern version reduces the original 1755 edition's 2,300 pages of definitions and literary examples to a more manageable length, retaining the verbal pleasure and historical curiosity of the original. 480pp. 5⅜₁₆ x 8¼. 0-486-44089-3

ADVENTURES OF HUCKLEBERRY FINN, Mark Twain, Illustrated by E. W. Kemble. A work of eternal richness and complexity, a source of ongoing critical debate, and a literary landmark, Twain's 1885 masterpiece about a barefoot boy's journey of self-discovery has enthralled readers around the world. This handsome clothbound reproduction of the first edition features all 174 of the original black-and-white illustrations. 368pp. 5⅜ x 8½. 0-486-44322-1

STICKLEY CRAFTSMAN FURNITURE CATALOGS, Gustav Stickley and L. & J. G. Stickley. Beautiful, functional furniture in two authentic catalogs from 1910. 594 illustrations, including 277 photos, show settles, rockers, armchairs, reclining chairs, bookcases, desks, tables. 183pp. 6½ x 9¼. 0-486-23838-5

AMERICAN LOCOMOTIVES IN HISTORIC PHOTOGRAPHS: 1858 to 1949, Ron Ziel (ed.). A rare collection of 126 meticulously detailed official photographs, called "builder portraits," of American locomotives that majestically chronicle the rise of steam locomotive power in America. Introduction. Detailed captions. xi+129pp. 9 x 12. 0-486-27393-8

AMERICA'S LIGHTHOUSES: An Illustrated History, Francis Ross Holland, Jr. Delightfully written, profusely illustrated fact-filled survey of over 200 American lighthouses since 1716. History, anecdotes, technological advances, more. 240pp. 8 x 10¾. 0-486-25576-X

TOWARDS A NEW ARCHITECTURE, Le Corbusier. Pioneering manifesto by founder of "International School." Technical and aesthetic theories, views of industry, economics, relation of form to function, "mass-production split" and much more. Profusely illustrated. 320pp. 6⅛ x 9¼. (Available in U.S. only.) 0-486-25023-7

HOW THE OTHER HALF LIVES, Jacob Riis. Famous journalistic record, exposing poverty and degradation of New York slums around 1900, by major social reformer. 100 striking and influential photographs. 233pp. 10 x 7⅞. 0-486-22012-5

FRUIT KEY AND TWIG KEY TO TREES AND SHRUBS, William M. Harlow. One of the handiest and most widely used identification aids. Fruit key covers 120 deciduous and evergreen species; twig key 160 deciduous species. Easily used. Over 300 photographs. 126pp. 5⅜ x 8½. 0-486-20511-8

COMMON BIRD SONGS, Dr. Donald J. Borror. Songs of 60 most common U.S. birds: robins, sparrows, cardinals, bluejays, finches, more—arranged in order of increasing complexity. Up to 9 variations of songs of each species.
Cassette and manual 0-486-99911-4

ORCHIDS AS HOUSE PLANTS, Rebecca Tyson Northen. Grow cattleyas and many other kinds of orchids—in a window, in a case, or under artificial light. 63 illustrations. 148pp. 5⅜ x 8½. 0-486-23261-1

MONSTER MAZES, Dave Phillips. Masterful mazes at four levels of difficulty. Avoid deadly perils and evil creatures to find magical treasures. Solutions for all 32 exciting illustrated puzzles. 48pp. 8¼ x 11. 0-486-26005-4

MOZART'S DON GIOVANNI (DOVER OPERA LIBRETTO SERIES), Wolfgang Amadeus Mozart. Introduced and translated by Ellen H. Bleiler. Standard Italian libretto, with complete English translation. Convenient and thoroughly portable—an ideal companion for reading along with a recording or the performance itself. Introduction. List of characters. Plot summary. 121pp. 5¼ x 8½. 0-486-24944-1

FRANK LLOYD WRIGHT'S DANA HOUSE, Donald Hoffmann. Pictorial essay of residential masterpiece with over 160 interior and exterior photos, plans, elevations, sketches and studies. 128pp. 9¼ x 10¾. 0-486-29120-0

CATALOG OF DOVER BOOKS

LIGHT AND SHADE: A Classic Approach to Three-Dimensional Drawing, Mrs. Mary P. Merrifield. Handy reference clearly demonstrates principles of light and shade by revealing effects of common daylight, sunshine, and candle or artificial light on geometrical solids. 13 plates. 64pp. 5⅜ x 8½. 0-486-44143-1

ASTROLOGY AND ASTRONOMY: A Pictorial Archive of Signs and Symbols, Ernst and Johanna Lehner. Treasure trove of stories, lore, and myth, accompanied by more than 300 rare illustrations of planets, the Milky Way, signs of the zodiac, comets, meteors, and other astronomical phenomena. 192pp. 8⅜ x 11. 0-486-43981-X

JEWELRY MAKING: Techniques for Metal, Tim McCreight. Easy-to-follow instructions and carefully executed illustrations describe tools and techniques, use of gems and enamels, wire inlay, casting, and other topics. 72 line illustrations and diagrams. 176pp. 8¼ x 10⅞. 0-486-44043-5

MAKING BIRDHOUSES: Easy and Advanced Projects, Gladstone Califf. Easy-to-follow instructions include diagrams for everything from a one-room house for bluebirds to a forty-two-room structure for purple martins. 56 plates; 4 figures. 80pp. 8¾ x 6⅜. 0-486-44183-0

LITTLE BOOK OF LOG CABINS: How to Build and Furnish Them, William S. Wicks. Handy how-to manual, with instructions and illustrations for building cabins in the Adirondack style, fireplaces, stairways, furniture, beamed ceilings, and more. 102 line drawings. 96pp. 8¾ x 6⅜. 0-486-44259-4

THE SEASONS OF AMERICA PAST, Eric Sloane. From "sugaring time" and strawberry picking to Indian summer and fall harvest, a whole year's activities described in charming prose and enhanced with 79 of the author's own illustrations. 160pp. 8¼ x 11. 0-486-44220-9

THE METROPOLIS OF TOMORROW, Hugh Ferriss. Generous, prophetic vision of the metropolis of the future, as perceived in 1929. Powerful illustrations of towering structures, wide avenues, and rooftop parks–all features in many of today's modern cities. 59 illustrations. 144pp. 8¼ x 11. 0-486-43727-2

THE PATH TO ROME, Hilaire Belloc. This 1902 memoir abounds in lively vignettes from a vanished time, recounting a pilgrimage on foot across the Alps and Apennines in order to "see all Europe which the Christian Faith has saved." 77 of the author's original line drawings complement his sparkling prose. 272pp. 5⅜ x 8½. 0-486-44001-X

THE HISTORY OF RASSELAS: Prince of Abissinia, Samuel Johnson. Distinguished English writer attacks eighteenth-century optimism and man's unrealistic estimates of what life has to offer. 112pp. 5⅜ x 8½. 0-486-44094-X

A VOYAGE TO ARCTURUS, David Lindsay. A brilliant flight of pure fancy, where wild creatures crowd the fantastic landscape and demented torturers dominate victims with their bizarre mental powers. 272pp. 5⅜ x 8½. 0-486-44198-9

Paperbound unless otherwise indicated. Available at your book dealer, online at **www.doverpublications.com**, or by writing to Dept. GI, Dover Publications, Inc., 31 East 2nd Street, Mineola, NY 11501. For current price information or for free catalogs (please indicate field of interest), write to Dover Publications or log on to **www.doverpublications.com** and see every Dover book in print. Dover publishes more than 500 books each year on science, elementary and advanced mathematics, biology, music, art, literary history, social sciences, and other areas.